For Mum and Dad
with all my love
~BC

First U.S. edition published in 2002 by
Barron's Educational Series, Inc.
250 Wireless Blvd, Hauppauge, NY 11788
www.barronseduc.com

First published in Great Britain 2002 by
Little Tiger Press
An imprint of Magi Publications

Text and Illustrations © 2002, Ben Cort. Reprinted by arrangement with
Barron's Educational Series, Inc., Hauppauge, NY.

Library of Congress No. 2001098219
International Standard Book No. 0-7641-5532-6

Printed in China
9 8 7 6 5 4 3 2 1

Ben Cort

PIGS CAN'T FLY!

Pig was feeling fed up. "I'm bored,"
he moaned. "Bored, bored, bored, bored,
bored! There must be something to do
that's fun and I'm
going to find it!"
So off he trotted.

Giraffe was grazing on the leaves at the top of the trees. Pig gazed up at him. "I bet exciting things happen to giraffes," he sighed. Suddenly, Pig had a clever idea!

Pig made some stilts. Then he went for a walk to try them out.

"Hello down there," Pig called to Zebra. "I'm a giraffe and it's great. I can see for miles."
"You're not a giraffe," laughed Zebra. "You're a wobbly pig on stilts, and you'd better be very careful."
Pig hobbled off in a huff, but he didn't get very far . . .

CRASH!

"Oh dear," Pig sighed as he dusted himself
off "A giraffe's life might not be for me.
What I really need is to look more exciting
– then I might find adventure!"
Pig had barely taken two steps when
he thought of another clever idea!

He got out his paints, and gave himself a wonderful new coat. Then he went for a run, to show it off.

"Hello there!" Pig said to Elephant. "I'm a zebra and it's great. I have stripes."
"You're not a zebra," laughed Elephant. "You're a stripy painted pig – but not for long . . ."

WHOOSH!

Pig spluttered in dismay as his beautiful coat washed away.

"Gee!" he sighed. "Being a zebra is worse than being a pig! I'm sure that being an elephant is much more fun . . ." And before Pig had even dried off, he'd thought up another clever idea!

P ig tied a long hose to his nose,
and some great big leaves to his ears.
Then off he stomped to try them out.

"Hello there," Pig said to Kangaroo.
"I'm an elephant and it's great.
I can squirt water with my trunk."
"You're not an elephant," laughed
Kangaroo. "You're a pig with
a hose on your nose."
Pig was about to disagree when . . .

ACHHOOO!

Off blew Pig's hose with
an enormous sneeze!

"Hmmpphh!" humphed Pig.
"Being an elephant isn't any fun either!
But being a kangaroo would surely be fun."
Just then, Pig had yet another clever idea.

Pig tied some super-springy
springs to his feet.
Off he bounced to try them out.

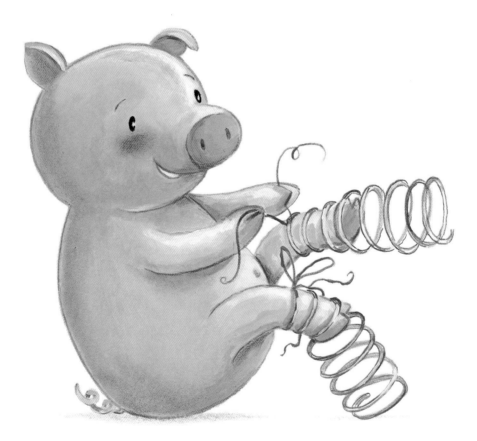

"Hello there!" Pig said to Parrot.
"I'm a kangaroo and it's great.
I can jump as high as a house."
"You're *not* a kangaroo," squawked
Parrot. "You're a silly pig on springs,
and you can't bounce very high."
Pig was so hopping mad at
Parrot's words that he bounced
higher . . . and higher . . .

until he bounced right up
into a tree, and got stuck!
Pig wiggled and wriggled.
"If only I could fly," he huffed
as he scrambled back down.
This gave Pig his cleverest
idea of all!

Pig found some feathers and
a shell, and he made himself
some wings and a great big beak.
Off he flapped to test them out.

"Hello there!" Pig said to Monkey. "I'm a parrot and it's great. I can fly as far as the eye can see."
"You're not a parrot," laughed Monkey. "You're a fluffy feathery pig, and pigs can't fly."

Monkey was right. Pig plunged like a stone into the mud below! "It's not fair!" he cried as he lay slap bang in the middle of the puddle. "Everything always goes wrong. Pigs never have any fun!"

But just then, a voice beside him called out . . .

"What do you mean, pigs never have any fun? I'm a pig and I have lots of fun rolling around in the mud. Try it!" So Pig rolled round and round . . .

and the more he rolled, the muckier he got, and the muckier he got, the more he liked it.

"Hoorah!" Pig squealed in delight.

"Being a pig is the most fun of all!"